THE BABY

A Red Fox Book

Published by Random House Children's Books
20 Vauxhall Bridge Road, London SW1V 2SA

A division of Random House UK Ltd
London Melbourne Sydney Auckland
Johannesburg and agencies throughout the world

1 3 5 7 9 10 8 6 4 2

First published in Great Britain by Jonathan Cape Ltd 1974

Red Fox edition 1995

Typeset by SX Composing Ltd, Rayleigh, Essex

Printed and bound in Hong Kong

RANDOM HOUSE UK Limited Reg. No. 954009

ISBN 0 09 950471 5

THE BABY
John Burningham

Red Fox

There is a baby
in our house

The baby makes a mess with its food

We take it for rides
in the pram

Sometimes I help Mummy bath the baby

The baby sleeps
in a cot

Sometimes I like
the baby

Sometimes I don't

It can't play
with me yet

I hope the baby

grows up soon

Little Books
by John Burningham

THE BABY

THE RABBIT

THE SCHOOL

THE SNOW

THE DOG

THE BLANKET

THE FRIEND

THE CUPBOARD